To Colton
From Bacon & Bacon
xoxo
Enjoy this book.
July 1/2012

TALES FROM THE

TOY
BOX

HELLO!

Humphrey Barchester Barrington, B.E.A.R. (RETD.) here. *Ahem!* My friends in the toy box have asked me to say a few words on their behalf to welcome you to this splendid collection of our stories. Now, I don't know if you realize how old some of us are, but we toys have all been played with and loved by many human children in our time—perhaps some could have been your parents, your grandparents, or even your great-grandparents—and we all have a tale to tell.

What do you think happens when the right bear goes to the wrong child, or a china doll gets into the wrong paws? Can a rocking horse ever gallop in green fields, or a lopsided bunny with no clothes and not enough stuffing find someone to love? And is it really possible that a toy could actually help to save a human being?

Read our stories to find the answers to these questions and to share our adventures. You may never look at your own old toys in the same way again.

TALES FROM THE
TOY
BOX

Written by
NICOLA BAXTER

Illustrated by
JENNY PRESS

ARMADILLO

Published by Armadillo Books
an imprint of
Bookmart Limited
Registered Number 2372865
Trading as Bookmart Limited
Desford Road
Enderby
Leicester
LE9 5AD

ISBN 1-90046-551-5

Produced for Bookmart Limited by Nicola Baxter
PO Box 215
Framingham Earl
Norwich Norfolk
NR14 7UR

Designer: Amanda Hawkes
Production designer: Amy Barton

Printed in Italy

CONTENTS

The Teddy Bear's Story of

THE CUDDLIEST FRIEND

told by

HUMPHREY BARCHESTER BARRINGTON, B.E.A.R. (RETD.)

WHAT IS THE WORST THING that can happen to a bear, my friends? It isn't ear-chewing or nose-nibbling or being pulled around by your paws. All human children do those things. No, the worst thing that can happen to a bear is to be unloved. And that is what once happened to me.

In the days when I was young, I was owned by a little girl called Lucy, and from the very first, I was a disappointment. She wanted a cuddly friend with a bow around his neck, not a fine, upstanding, naval bear like myself. When her nurse took her to the park to play, we often met other nurses and their children. When she saw a handsome, furry bear, Lucy would sigh. I knew she was wishing that I could be more like him.

One day, I had the opportunity to meet just such a bear. His name was Binkie. I'm not usually … *ahem* … a bear to show his deepest feelings, but there was something about Binkie that made me want to tell him everything. Before long, I had told him how upset I was that my little owner didn't really love me.

"She doesn't do anything unkind, you know," I told him, "but I'm sure she would be quite happy if she never saw me again. I try to keep my chin up, but I feel I'm failing in my duty as a bear."

To my surprise, Binkie began to laugh.

"My friend," he chuckled, "what a curious coincidence that I have met you here today. I am owned by a little boy called Oscar. He has never liked me from the day I was given to him by his aunt. He thinks he is too old for a cuddly bear with a ribbon around his neck. He prefers trains and building bricks. Even when we are alone at night he never talks to me. But I think he might like a fine, upstanding, naval bear very well. You can guess what I am thinking!"

I could, of course, but it seemed a very dangerous undertaking. Lucy's nurse, although she was, in my view, a very silly woman, might easily notice if Binkie and I exchanged places. And you can never tell with those females what they are going to make a fuss about. Why, I went for the tiniest little sail in a toy boat on the pool in the park once, and that woman jumped up and down shrieking as if it was Lucy herself out on the water.

Still, Binkie's idea was very tempting.

"By Jove," I declared. "All right, I'll jolly well do it! What is your plan, Binkie?"

Binkie looked blank for a long moment. I began to fear that a fluffy outside might point to a fluffy brain *inside*. But Binkie was soon outlining a sensible plan.

"What we need," he said, "is for the children to think of the idea of a swap themselves. Their nurses won't be able to say no if both Lucy and Oscar are shouting. You go and play with Oscar, and I will make friends with Lucy. Good luck!"

"Good luck, old man," I replied gruffly.

Lucy was picking flowers from one of the park borders while the nurses chatted. It was strictly forbidden to pick the flowers, and I wouldn't have done it myself, but I noticed that Binkie went over and handed Lucy a daisy in a very charming manner. That bear certainly had a way with the ladies.

Oscar was playing with a toy train on the path. I sat down nearby until he noticed me and lifted me into one of the trucks that the little engine pulled. It was a tight fit for my poor legs. These days my stuffing isn't what it was, but then I had firm, plump legs. My paws were sore for a long while after.

Oscar chuffed the train up and down the path.

"You can be the conductor," he said to me. "Blow your whistle when it is time for the train to start. It's a pity I haven't got a little green flag for you to wave."

Quick as a flash, I took a leaf out of Binkie's book. Well, actually, I took a leaf out of the flower border, but you know what I mean. The large green leaf looked a lot like a flag. When Oscar whistled, I waved it in the air. He clapped his little hands in delight.

All too soon, it was time to go home.

"Give Oscar back his bear, Lucy," said Lucy's nurse.

"Give Lucy back her bear, Oscar," said Oscar's nurse.

And the two little mites cried out together, "No!" and held their new bears tight.

I hadn't been squeezed like that since I'd gone to Lucy's house, so it quite took my breath away.

The nurses looked at each other helplessly.

"Well, Lucy's is a very nice bear," said Oscar's nurse at last. "I suppose no one will mind if you just borrow it for a while."

Lucy's nurse agreed.

"To tell you the truth," she said, lowering her voice, "Lucy's parents don't take much notice of what she does or which toys she plays with. They are always busy going to meetings. I don't think it will matter if the sailor bear never comes home."

When I heard that, I must confess that I looked at young Lucy with new eyes. I had always thought she was a little girl who had everything, but now I wasn't so sure. Oscar's nurse was speaking as I turned back towards her.

"Oscar's parents are the same," she said. "His father is often away at sea, and his mother spends all her time doing what she calls good works. Mostly, that means she takes soup to poor people. I don't call that a good work myself. The soup, I happen to know, is *horrible*."

Binkie coughed and shuffled his feet. We both realized at the same time that it was not surprising our owners did not cuddle or care for us. No one did much cuddling or caring of *them*!

Without saying a word, Binkie and I silently went back to our real owners. Binkie clasped his arms around little Oscar's leg and hugged him. I piled some more flowers in Lucy's lap, and I bowed very respectfully as I did it. In the end, neither of the children complained when they went home with their own bears that evening.

My friends, I learnt a valuable lesson that day. I had been feeling unhappy because I wasn't loved, but all the time, I wasn't loving anyone myself. As soon as I did that, Lucy and I started being the best of friends. *Ahem* ... I'm still not much of a bear for showing my feelings, but I still love that little girl today—and, I hope it won't be betraying a confidence to tell you—that little girl was seventy-three today. And she still loves flowers!

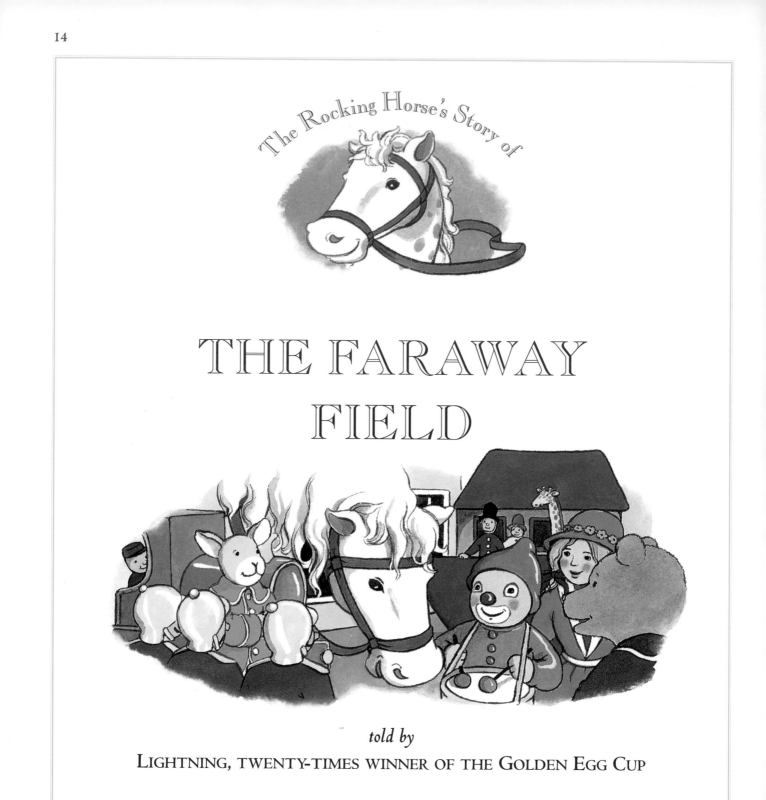

The Rocking Horse's Story of

THE FARAWAY FIELD

told by

LIGHTNING, TWENTY-TIMES WINNER OF THE GOLDEN EGG CUP

HE HE HE-HE-HE, HA HA! Sorry, it's a nervous habit. I'm not really laughing at you, Teddy Bear. Ha ha, oh no. He he. It's just that with all of you looking at me, you know, I feel a bit nervous. He he he! I'd better get on with my story. Oh dear. He he, ha ha!

Once upon a time, there was a rocking horse. He he. A rocking horse a lot like me. He was terribly good looking, with a long mane and a tail that flew in the breeze when he galloped. He he. And how he could gallop! He was the fastest galloper in the whole wide world.

What's that? Well, yes, he he, that's true. He didn't know for sure he was the fastest galloper in the world because he had never met another horse—even another rocking horse. You don't, you see, if you are inside a house. It's different for bears and dolls. Sometimes they get taken outside for picnics and parties. Horses are too big for that kind of thing.

The horse in this story used to look out of the window of his boy's bedroom. Far, far away, beyond the garden and the lane, he could see a green field. More than anything in the world, he wanted to gallop on that smooth, fresh grass.

It wasn't, you can be sure, that the rocking horse didn't get enough exercise. The boy and his friends loved to ride. And the older they got, the faster the rocking horse had to gallop. Pretty soon, the boys discovered that if they rocked really hard, the horse would move along the carpet. That was when they started the Golden Egg Cup Races.

The boys had heard that a horse race often had a cup as the prize. They tried to borrow an expensive vase from downstairs that was just the right shape, but one of the grown-ups stopped them. He he. Then they found an old egg cup with ducks painted on it. With a coat of rather drippy yellow paint it became the Golden Egg Cup.

Yes, I won … I mean, the horse in this story won, he he, the Golden Egg Cup lots and lots of times. It wasn't very difficult when the other riders only had a baby's push-along puppy and a toddler's little tricycle to ride on.

But even winning the Golden Egg Cup twenty times didn't make the rocking horse happy. He still looked out of the window at the green field and longed to gallop across it.

Then, one day, when the rocking horse looked out he saw something wonderful. There were real horses in the field! Three animals were running and jumping on a windy spring day. They kicked up their heels and tossed their heads in the sunshine.

The rocking horse couldn't bear it any more. He felt a kind of sad, lonely feeling in his wooden heart. He decided there and then to make his dream come true.

That night, the rocking horse waited until everyone was asleep. Then, very slowly at first, he began to rock.

Luckily, the bedroom door was open. Silently, across the carpet, the rocking horse rocked his way across the room and out into the hall. It was a place he had never been before. At the end of the patterned carpet, he saw something that frightened him. A broad flight of stairs led down to the entrance hall below.

Now the rocking horse had never seen stairs before. He had certainly never tried to go up or down them. Slowly, he rocked to the top of the flight and looked down. It seemed a very, very long way. It seemed very, very steep.

The rocking horse thought about the Egg Cup Races and his life in the boy's room. He thought about the three horses running free in the green field. He decided that he had no choice.

The rocking horse counted to four (which is as far as he could count). Then he counted to four again. He was just about to count to four for a third time, when the big clock behind him struck twelve.

Boing!

The rocking horse lurched forward.

Boing!

The rocking horse felt his rockers slipping underneath him.

Boing!

The rocking horse flew down the stairs, faster than he had ever galloped before, and...

Crash!

He landed at the bottom, tumbled nose over tail, and ended up just inside the front door.

The whole household came running. It took a moment for the boy to recognize that the jumble of wood lying on the floor was his champion racer.

The rocking horse was so dazed, he could hardly think. He certainly didn't know what a bad state he was in. A deep voice sounded high above him.

"He's too badly broken to mend, Tom. I'll get Jim to carry the bits out to the woodshed. I can't think how this could have happened. It's a shame."

So the rocking horse lay in the woodshed. Weeks passed. Months passed. Years passed. In the gloomy shed, the rocking horse closed his eyes and dreamed of the green field. There was nothing else to do.

"Well, well, well. What have we here?" A deep voice was speaking over the rocking horse once more, but this one was different. An old man stooped over the jumble of wood and picked up a few pieces.

"It's all here!" he exclaimed. "This will keep me busy this winter."

In the workshop at the end of the woodshed, as the snow fell outside, the old man slowly put the rocking horse together again. The day came when he once again stood on his rockers and looked about him. He needed painting. He needed his mane and tail to be combed and clipped, but he looked fine.

"Now," said the old man, when his work was finished at last, "I never had a rocking horse when I was a boy, but I reckon it's not too late. We need to find somewhere private, though. I don't think my daughter will see this as a dignified way for me to spend my time. Come on, Lightning. That's what I'm going to call you."

The old man carried the horse out of the shed and down the lane, to a green field where the spring breezes blew. He he. Ha ha. I don't know why I'm crying, my friends. It was such a happy day and such a long time ago. You just never know when dreams will come true.

The China Doll's Story of

THE RED RIBBONS

told by
EMMELINE APRIL FLORINDA FAY

NOW THEN, YOU TOYS! Just because I'm a china doll, some people think I must be shy and silly. Well, I'm not at all. It's true that I have to take care of myself. It would be hard to mend *me* if I fell down the stairs, Rocking Horse. But I'm not as fragile as I look, as my story will show.

Like most of you, I was bought as a present for a child. Her name was Patience, which made me laugh. A less patient child you never have met. The first morning she played with me, she dropped me twice, sat on me once and stood on my head when I wouldn't talk to her. Well, you know as well as I do the rules about that.

Now, it was lucky that Patience's mother walked into the room just as her daughter was about to do dreadful damage to me.

"Patience Parker!" she cried. "Give me that beautiful doll! You are obviously not old enough to take care of her properly. I will look after her until you become more sensible!"

I was expecting to be put away in a cupboard, but I was wrong. It turned out that Mrs. Parker didn't have dolls to play with when she was young. Now she played with me! Yes, she really did. At night, she combed my hair and changed my clothes. Her husband laughed but she didn't mind. She said I was like the pretty little girl she had always wanted.

"Patience is pretty!" her husband protested, but he admitted that his daughter wasn't very interested in dolls or clothes or cooking—the kinds of things that girls were meant to like in those days.

"*She* wouldn't let me put ribbons in her hair like this," sighed Mrs. Parker, tying lots of little red bows in my hair.

Mrs. Parker looked after me so well that I really didn't want to be given back to impatient Patience. Still, every so often her mother thought she should try.

"Look, darling!" she'd say. "Here's your beautiful doll. Wouldn't you like to play with her now?"

Patience would grunt and go back to her model aeroplanes.

"Not really," she'd say.

Well, time passed. Patience stopped wanting to be a pilot and started planning to become a mountaineer. Then she thought she would try deep-sea diving. All of her enthusiasms lasted for a few weeks. Then model aeroplanes, ropes and goggles were thrown into a cupboard and she was on to the next thing. She never showed the slightest bit of interest in me.

Unfortunately, the time came when Mrs. Parker began to neglect me, too. It was all because of Fluffykins. Ugh! That wasn't the silly dog's real name, but it was what Mrs. Parker called him. That and Honeybunny, Pompom, Mummy's Ickle Darling and other horrible names. He was a Pekinese. His hair, I must confess, was as long and silky as mine. Naturally, it wasn't long before Mrs. Parker began putting ribbons in it—red ones.

I was upset when no one seemed to notice me any more. I sat on a shelf in Mrs. Parker's bedroom and my dress grew dusty. Then, to my horror, someone *did* notice me. It was that wretched dog!

One day when he was waiting for his mistress to come home, Fluffykins wandered into the room, jumped up onto a chair and reached me on my shelf. He seized me in his horrible teeth and shook me! I could feel my dress tearing and my hair flopping everywhere. I was really frightened.

The next thing I knew, I was being carried down the stairs and out into the garden. Then I was even more frightened. You hear about dogs burying things, don't you? I didn't want to be buried. I couldn't think of what to do, until one of the bows fell out of my hair and on to the grass. After that, I dropped more ribbons on purpose as we sped along.

I can hardly bring myself to tell you where that puppy left me. It was on the compost heap—the smelliest spot in the garden.

It was a whole day later that Mrs. Parker noticed I was missing at last. "Burglars!" she cried—I could hear it all the way down the garden. I could hear the soothing tones of Mr. Parker calming her down, as well.

I might have been there for ever, but young Patience heard the mention of burglars and became very interested. Her latest wish was to be a detective. She soon spotted my red-ribbon trail and followed it to the … well, to my hiding place. Then she carried me proudly into the house.

After that, Patience took notice of me at last. She put me on a shelf with her magnifying glass, all the red ribbons and a notebook in which she kept a record of all the crimes she solved. So, you see, because of my clever plan, she came to care for me at last. For me, only one mystery remained. What did the big notice she put around my neck mean?

THE CIRCUS SURPRISE

told by

COCO TUMBLETRICK

HEY, TOYS! LISTEN TO THIS ONE! What do you get if you peel two bananas? A pair of slippers! And what about this one? Oh, you don't want to hear it? But clowns love to make people laugh. My jokes don't make you laugh? Well, I'm going to sulk in the corner and not tell you a story then. Oh, you *do* want a story? Okay. My story is about what happens when humans forget you, too.

You all know that I'm a clockwork clown. Wind me up and I'll play my little drum and jiggle a bit and then fall flat on my nose. Yes, I know it's a big nose, Rocking Horse. You don't have to go on about it. Anyway, some clockwork toys have their winding keys in their backs, so they have to be wound up by someone else. I'm lucky. My key is in my side, so I can wind myself up. Of course, I never let human beings know about that. They don't even know we can talk, do they?

Now, just like the China Doll and you, Rocking Horse, I've been loved by children and I've been lost by children. With me, it happened when my family moved house. They lived in a great big, rambling house with lots of rooms. On the day when the servants began to pack everything up, the baby threw me into a dark corner. No one noticed I was there.

When the last load of boxes was carted away, and the house was quiet, I was still sitting in my corner. I felt very, very lonely. Soon, it began to grow dark.

Now, we all know that houses seem different at night. But an empty house is very strange. I wasn't worried when I heard the odd creak. All houses do that as they settle down for the night. But when I began to hear rustlings and scamperings and squeakings, I became very worried indeed. Obviously, there were other living things in the house as well, and I wasn't quite sure what they were.

Around midnight, I heard the church clock strike from across the garden. Just at that moment, a shaft of moonlight gleamed through the window and I saw ... twenty pairs of bright little eyes watching me!

I must have gasped or something because the next thing I knew, a little squeaky voice was saying, "It's alive!"

She scuttled forward in the moonlight, and I realized that she was a mouse!

They were all mice! Now if I had been made of wood, like you, Rocking Horse, I would have been very frightened. Everyone knows that mice can nibble and mice can gnaw. But my tin body is tough—a little dented, perhaps, but definitely too hard for a mouse to munch.

"What is it?" asked another squeaky voice, coming closer. Soon I was surrounded by a mass of little furry bodies. They peered at me. They sniffed at me. They twitched their little whiskers at me. Although I knew they couldn't hurt me, I didn't like it very much.

"It's not much use," squealed a small mouse near my left ear. "We can't eat it and it doesn't *do* anything."

"I certainly do!" I cried, and they all jumped back in surprise. I mean, a self-respecting clown can't just sit there and let mice insult him! I decided it was time for a demonstration.

Slowly and carefully, I turned my key around and around. It made a kind of whirring noise that the mice didn't like very much.

They watched from a distance. Then, when I was ready, I stopped winding and...

Da da da da, da-di-da, da da, da-di-da, da da, da-di-da!

I began playing my little drum as loudly and as quickly as I could. The sound was huge in the quiet house. When I looked up, not a single mouse could be seen.

"Well, well, well," I said to myself. "Now I know how to get rid of *them*! That's good."

Well, it was good for a little while, but it wasn't long before I was feeling lonely again. I had no one to talk to. I had no one to play my little drum for. I had no one to fall on my nose for. I love to hear my audience laugh.

Even the mice were better than no one. But the mice did not return. They were obviously too frightened.

I had plenty of time to think about what to do. In the end, I decided that I must show those mice there was nothing to be afraid of. So I wound myself up, over and over again, and played my little drum to the empty house.

It worked! On the second night, I saw little noses twitching in the corners. Bright little eyes came nearer and nearer.

"Don't be afraid," I said. "I'm a clown!"

Now, you can't imagine what the leader mouse said next. I could hardly believe my ears.

"What's a clown?" he asked.

Well, everyone knows what a clown is, surely! I was wrong. These poor mice had never heard of the circus or clowns.

For the next few days, when the sun went down and the mice came out to play, I told them stories about the circus. I told them my jokes, too, but they didn't laugh very much. Don't say anything, Rocking Horse! I can see what you're thinking!

Well, those mice started whispering in corners and disappearing into other rooms. All I could hear were a lot of squeaks and thuds. Later, I noticed that some mice were limping and some were no longer talking to each other, but I didn't guess what they were doing.

As a matter of fact, I was getting a bit sad again. I mean, mice are fine animals, when you get to know them, but they don't know very much. By the time I'd told them all my circus stories, we didn't have much else to talk about. I longed to belong to a child again and join in all the fun of the nursery.

Then, one day, some visitors came to the house. They were clearly a couple thinking of buying it. And they seemed to like what they saw.

"This room will be perfect for our youngest," I heard the woman say. "And look, someone has even left a toy here. You know how he loves clowns. I think it's a sign."

As they left, I heard her husband saying that they would like to move in within the month.

Now it was the mice's turn to look glum.

"We'll have to find somewhere else to live," they said. "Humans don't like us in their houses. But before we go, dear clown, we have a surprise for you. *Da daaaa!*"

And to my surprise, little mice came tumbling from every side, some doing acrobatics, some pretending to be clowns, some swinging on the light cord. A little band of them even made music with straw pipes and cotton-reel drums.

You know, it was the best circus performance I've ever seen. People can surprise you. Toys can surprise you. And, sometimes, even mice can surprise you! I love surprises. Don't you?

Mr. Noah's Story of

THE ADVENTUROUS ELEPHANT

told by

MR. NOAH, ANIMALS AFLOAT, INC.

MICE? DON'T TALK TO ME ABOUT MICE! On the Ark, the first Mr. Noah, who began the company years ago, started off with two of them and ended up with hundreds! He had trouble with a lot of the animals, but he didn't have my problem. When he was floating about for forty days and forty nights in the pouring rain, even the silliest animals didn't try to leave the Ark. My story is about one of my elephants, who simply hasn't got the sense to stay where she belongs.

Now, if you ask any child about the animals in the Ark, she knows one thing. The animals went in two by two. You can see for yourselves that I have two giraffes, two hippos, two ostriches, two crocodiles, two monkeys, and so on. I even have two elephants, but it wasn't always that way, as I'll tell you.

My Ark has always been a popular toy. Little ones love to play with it. When I was brand new and all my paint was shiny, I was even put on display in the toy shop window. They made a kind of scene, with a green hill for the Ark to sit on, a big rainbow arching overhead, and all the animals coming down the gangplank. It looked wonderful. But right away there was trouble.

One day a woman came into the shop to buy me. She wore an enormous hat, I remember, with feathers and things. The shopkeeper kept hopping about anxiously, thinking she might knock his toy soldiers off the shelf. She didn't waste words.

"I want that Noah's Ark," she said. "Please wrap it while I finish my shopping."

Of course, the shopkeeper got to work at once. But he was very busy that morning, so he gave the packing to his young assistant to finish. Later that morning, I was collected and carried to the posh lady's house.

Two hours later, I was back in the shop, feeling sure the other toys were all laughing at me.

"When I buy a toy, my good man," said the lady in the big hat, "I expect it to be complete. What do you mean by this?"

There were a lot of red faces and confusion. At last it became clear that one of the elephants was missing. The poor little assistant was sure it had been in the package that morning. The lady was very upset about this and insisted on his dismissal. It was all most unpleasant.

Naturally, the shopkeeper was anxious to keep his customer happy. The assistant had to search every inch of the shop in search of the missing elephant. It was nowhere to be found.

"This is a disgrace!" cried the customer, as she swept out of the shop. "I have wasted half a day and still have no present for my grandson. I shall be taking my custom elsewhere in future."

I think the shopkeeper was probably secretly glad about that but he still had a problem. A Noah's Ark without all its animals never does seem right. He knew he wouldn't be able to sell it in that state.

After another search failed to find the missing elephant, the shopkeeper was in a terrible state. Even he was beginning to blame the assistant, when the lad had a bright idea.

"If you take away the other elephant," he said. "There will still be two of everything else. No one will notice."

It seemed like a good plan at the time...

Only two days later, a man brought his small son into the shop and asked right away to see the Noah's Ark in the window. Piece by piece, we were brought out on to the counter. The little boy sat up beside us and beamed when he saw all the animals.

"One happy customer," laughed the man. "We'll take it!"

Even as he said it, the little boy's face became worried and pale. "No, Dad," he said. "I don't want it!"

"But it's just what you wanted," his father protested. "Really, Josh, what is it you want now?"

"I still want an Ark," sniffed the boy. "But it's got to have effelants."

"Effelants? Of course it's got effelants, I mean elephants," said his father. "All Noah's Arks have elephants."

Although the shopkeeper tried hard to persuade the man that Arks without elephants were the latest thing, he did not manage to sell us.

"I have to say I agree with my son," said the man. "An Ark without elephants, indeed! What a ridiculous idea!"

Now the shopkeeper didn't know what to do. He wondered if he could find someone to carve another elephant to match the first. Until he could do so, he took the Ark out of the window and put it away in his storeroom.

We've heard from other toys today about how they sometimes get forgotten. I stayed in that dusty storeroom, with boxes of purple teddy bears that no one wanted and various toys with damaged boxes or missing labels. It was a miserable time. How angry I was about that wretched elephant! After all, it was her fault we were in this mess. My wife agreed with me. Each day she counted all the other animals just to make sure matters were not getting worse.

One morning, over a year later, my wife woke me from a very pleasant snooze by shouting in my ear. I wasn't too pleased.

"Noah!" she cried. "She's back!"

It took me ages to understand what she was talking about. You can't wake a busy man and expect him to have all his wits about him straight away. When I finally understood that she meant the missing elephant had returned, I couldn't believe it.

"Are you sure?" I demanded. "One elephant looks much like another, you know."

"But there are *two!*" cried my wife. "Of course, I'm sure!" And I'm afraid she added something regrettable about lazy business-owners who sleep their lives away, leaving other people to do their work for them. I ignored all that nonsense.

And Mrs. Noah was right. Standing peacefully outside the Ark, looking as if they had been there for months, were two elephants.

"I'm going to give that adventurous elephant a piece of my mind," I said.

"Which one?" asked Mrs. Noah. "You said yourself that one elephant looks much like another. It wouldn't be fair to be angry with the one that has been here all the time."

She was right, but it made me even crosser. I called all the animals together and gave them a lecture on their responsibilities as toys and employees of Animals Afloat, Inc. Mrs. Noah says I bored them all to sleep and it was several weeks later that we were packed up and taken away. I say it was that very same day. In any case, the shopkeeper was obviously tired of seeing us sitting on the shelf. He didn't bother to count us before carrying us away. He donated us with five purple teddy bears and a doll with no hair to the children's ward at the local hospital. I have never seen boys and girls look so happy in my life.

Mrs. Noah says it was lucky that elephant wandered off. She says we would never have been so happy in a posh house with spoilt children. I don't like to say it, but she's right. Now, where is that silly crocodile?

The Toy Train's Story of

THE BROKEN BRIDGE

told by

DRIVER OF TOY TRAIN No. 17101996KMAB SPECIAL

SOME OF YOU, I know, think that the life of a toy train is not an exciting one. My engine and I don't get invited to picnics or cuddled by the children in bed at night. We can't even play with them in the bath, in case our wheels get rusty and our funnel fills up.

But I would like you to remember, toys, that the engine is faster than any of you. Yes, even faster than you, Rocking Horse! And we have had adventures out in the big, wide world that the rest of you have only dreamed of.

This story takes place a few summers ago, when my master built a huge track for us in the garden. It was wonderful! We zoomed under the trees and over a little bridge. Then we whizzed around the summer house and came back to the station near the swing. It was lovely to puff around the track and feel the breeze on my face. The birds in the trees peered down at us. Butterflies landed on our carriages. I have never felt so happy.

All that summer, my master played with us every day. Then, as the leaves began to turn brown, orange and red, something quite dreadful happened.

One night, a fierce wind came howling around the house. We were safe inside, of course, for my master was very careful to bring us in at night. We sat on the nursery windowsill and listened as the wind rattled the window panes.

Next morning, the garden looked dreadful. Almost all the leaves had been blown from the trees. The grass was covered with twigs.

"Driver," said my master, "it is time to close the line for the winter. The wind has dropped and the sun is shining. We will make one last trip. I want top speed from you!"

I was happy to agree. Some drivers are cautious with their engines. They puff them along their tracks as slowly as snails crawling along a leaf. But an engine—a real engine—is built for speed! What is life if you can't whizz? I oiled the pistons and polished the coachwork. I was determined that our last trip of the season should be the fastest yet.

Outside, the boy put us on the track. "All aboard!" he called. He blew his whistle and waved his flag. We were off!

Over the rails the engine's wheels flew. Jiggly jiggly, jiggly jiggly. As we flashed under the trees, we picked up speed. Jiggledy jiggle, jiggledy jiggle. Around the bend and past the pond. Jiggledy jig jig, jiggledy jig. We raced along in the bright, autumn air, the rails humming beneath us.

But as we rushed towards the bridge, I saw that something was very wrong. The rail ahead looked bent and buckled. I strained my eyes to see. As we hurtled on, I saw what had happened—too late to brake, too late to cry out to my master. A branch had been blown onto the line. The rails were twisted, but worse than that—where once there was a bridge, now there was only a sickening gap below.

Faster and faster we sped towards disaster. Too late, I pulled on the brake. Too late, I shouted at the top of my voice. All too soon, I felt a sickening lurch as the engine reached the twisted track. Then, as I clung to the controls, the engine left the rails and flew through the air.

It seemed that we were airborne for ever, but it can only have been for a few seconds. We sailed out through the bare branches of the trees and I shut my eyes, waiting for the crash that must surely come. Through my mind flashed images of twisted, broken metal. I had no time to think or feel.

Thud! The shock sent me flying from the cabin. *Thunk!* I landed on a soft bed! Next to me lay the engine. It was on its side, yes, but at first sight it looked completely undamaged.

When I had recovered from the shock, I looked around. We were lying on a kind of mattress made of twigs and dried grass and feathers. It took me a few more seconds—I must have been dazed by the crash—to realize that we had landed in a bird's nest! It seemed like a miracle!

You will think I was slow, but it was not until a few moments later that I realized the full horror of our situation. We were safe, yes, but we were also twenty feet up in a tree. It's a position in which no engine and no driver wishes to find himself.

There was worse to come. With a squawking and a scuffling, a big, shaggy bird arrived on the edge of the nest. I could tell she didn't think much of her visitors.

"Madam," I said, as politely as I could in the circumstances. "Please don't shuffle your feet like that. We could fall out! No! No, no! No flapping! And don't bounce that branch! We have an excellent sense of balance—on rails—but we are not at all used to bouncing."

The wretched bird put her head on one side and peered at us out of bright little eyes. I didn't like the look she gave us.

"We are not at all good to eat," I said firmly. The bird decided not to believe me. She took a quite unnecessary peck at my plumpest parts and I'm sorry to say that I bear the marks to this day. There's no need to stare, Baby Doll.

Over the days that followed, I had plenty of time to think about the predicament in which we found ourselves. An engine is a magnificent machine, but it cannot climb trees. And a loyal driver ... *ahem* ... never leaves his engine (especially if he is not too keen on heights).

Time passed. The weather grew colder. The bird spent most of her time huddled up on her nest. Sometimes she was joined by her mate. They really were the untidiest birds. It wasn't long before my cabin was filled with feathers. I don't like to tell you what the funnel was filled with.

Then, one night, when steel clouds hid the stars, it began to snow. Soft, white, flakes, as soft as the bird's feathers but much, much colder, came falling through the bare branches. They covered the engine. They covered me. They even covered the sleeping bird. And as the nest began to look like a snow-covered pie, it also grew heavier and heavier.

Whooosh! Suddenly, we were falling, faster than a speeding engine, towards the white ground below. With a squawk, the bird woke up and flapped away, seconds before the moment when we hit the ground with a soft *thwump!*

No axles were broken. No funnels were bent. We had landed as safely on the ground as we had in the nest. But what would happen to us here on the ground? Hundreds of horrible possible happenings rushed through my head.

The next thing I heard was a shout of joy. Our master, building a snowman in the garden, had found us!

"Christmas has come early!" he laughed.

So that was the end of one of our many adventures. The only sad thing is that now we are carefully kept indoors all the time. How I would love to feel the wind in my wheels again! Well, never mind.

Robbie Rabbit's Story of

THE POOR,
BARE BUNNY

told by
ROBERT JAMES RABBIT ESQ.

MY FRIENDS, SEEING A PROSPEROUS, PLUMP RABBIT like myself before you, you may find it hard to imagine that not all rabbits are so fortunate. My story concerns a poor young rabbit who had a very hard start in life.

This rabbit, whom I shall call Jim, was made in a toy factory at the end of a long, hot Friday. The man who made him was tired and wanted to go home. He didn't pay the attention he should.

He simply tossed the finished rabbit into a basket with the others he had made that day and left his workbench.

Dear, dear. I say "finished rabbit", but really, the poor creature that lay on top of the pile looked very far from finished. His nose was not in the middle. One ear was bigger than the other. His eyes were lopsided. Worst of all— and you will shudder at this, toys—*he didn't have enough stuffing.* Yes, he was thin, a miserable, mis-shapen animal who disgraced the name of rabbit.

Well, a Friday afternoon is a Friday afternoon. The workman who made young Jim was not the only one to cut corners that day. The Controller, whose job it was to check the workmanship of all the toys made in the factory, skimped on her duties as well. She simply glanced at the rabbits in the basket, thinking all the time about her supper, and attached a red label that meant "Passed and approved".

That was that. The rabbits went down to the Packing Department, where the young lads who made up the packages had some cruel words to say and a good laugh at the expense of young Jim. They wrapped him up, with four other rabbits, and sent him overseas to a large toy shop that had a regular order.

The package did *not* arrive on a Friday afternoon. It was delivered on a Tuesday morning. No one was rushing off for the weekend. The person who opened the parcel at once shook his head, said, "This won't do!" and called for his manager.

There was no doubt in the manager's mind. The young rabbit must be sent back. "Not suitable for sale" wrote the manager on a label. He pinned the label to Jim's ear (some human beings have no idea how to treat a toy) and went straight to the telephone to make a complaint.

But the toy factory's manager was not very helpful. "We don't take back toys," he said. "What would we do with them? Look, I'll see what I can do about your bill. Why don't you put the rabbit into your next Sale and get rid of it like that?"

I want you to know, my friends, that poor young Jim heard every word of the conversation. Imagine how it hurt him to hear himself spoken of that way. It is not surprising that he sat down with his head in his paws and wished he had never been made.

Well, Jim was put on a shelf to wait for the Sale. Beside him were a china doll with a broken finger, a lead soldier with one leg, a drumming monkey who couldn't drum, a sailor doll with no hat, a teddy bear with a tear in his tummy, and a clown whose smile was upside down.

Here, at least, young Jim expected to get some sympathy. Surely a rabbit could expect other less-than-perfect toys to treat him kindly? I'm afraid not. As soon as the storeroom door was closed, the china doll began to laugh. The lead soldier joined in so heartily that he overbalanced. The teddy bear was soon giggling as well, which was silly of him because it simply made his stuffing come out.

Jim was upset. When the china doll turned up her nose and pointed out that he was not wearing any clothes, he understood why they were all laughing.

"A bare bunny!" screamed the clown. "What a joke! At least I'm fully clothed."

"Ooooh, don't," smirked the china doll. "You're making me blush. I can't look, really, I can't."

The young rabbit made up his mind there and then. At the very first opportunity, he slipped off the shelf and made his escape. He was out of the shop door and away down the street before you could say "Rabbit!"

Now bunnies may not be especially brave, or clever, or strong, but they are *fast*. Young Jim was off and out of the town in seconds. He soon found himself running across meadows full of flowers. Birds sang overhead. Butterflies fluttered around his head. For the first time in his short life, he felt happy.

Considering that Jim was a toy rabbit, not a real one, he did pretty well in the countryside. He found himself a home in a hollowed-out tree and didn't mind that it was already occupied by a spider, two beetles and a centipede.

But as summer passed, Jim found that he had made a big mistake. Real rabbits have waterproof fur and fill themselves with food to keep out the winter cold. Jim couldn't do that, and when the rain came, his fur and his stuffing became soggy. Jim didn't start out as a handsome rabbit, but he was a sorry sight indeed by the time that winter was over. His fur was muddy and matted. His ears were droopy and dull. He looked, to be frank, more like a rat than a rabbit.

Friends, it was then that Jim had an incredible piece of luck. It didn't seem like luck at the time, but it was. A little terrier dog, a yappy, annoying little creature, found Jim when out for a walk with his mistress.

"Put it down, Yaffles!" shrieked the lady. "What have you got there? Oh, put it down!" She probably thought Jim really *was* a rat!

But Yaffles was not a dog who was willing to let go of treasures that he found. He clenched his teeth around poor Jim and refused to put him down. Shuddering, the lady marched home, with Yaffles, looking proud and determined, padding along beside her.

Back at the lady's grand house, Yaffles was sent down to the basement to be cleaned up before he was allowed into the drawing room. The cook had a better idea of how to deal with a determined dog than her mistress. She made a suggestion to Yaffles. Yaffles thought it over. A second later, Yaffles was chewing a tasty bone, and the cook was gingerly holding what was left of poor Jim.

"There's no way of telling what you are," she said, "until you're cleaned up. Let's see what a bit of soap and water can do."

A bit of soap, a lot of water, and far too much use of the scrubbing brush later, Jim looked more like a rat than ever. The cook hung him up on the laundry line—by his ears!

And there, in the soft sunshine and a spring breeze, things began to get better for Jim. His fur dried out and looked fluffy and new. His ears lost their droop. His tail regained its fluffiness. When the cook took him down, she was smiling.

"Let me get my sewing kit, my lad," she said. "I'll soon have you fit to be seen."

And she did. She put his nose and his eyes straight. She adjusted his ears. She even tucked in a bit more stuffing. And she made that young rabbit the most beautiful green coat you've ever seen. Best of all, she gave him to a little girl who loved him. Young Jim's dreadful days were over.

What's that, China Doll? My coat? Nonsense! Just a coincidence. Nothing more. How could you think it? This *was* just a story, you know.

The Toy Soldier's Story of

THE LOVELY LADY

told by
PRIVATE BOGGLETHORPE, HER HIGHNESS'S HUSSARS

COME ON! COME ON! LOOK LIVELY! I've been waiting for ages to tell our story. My comrades have … *ahem!* … asked me to speak for them. Our story, you may be surprised to learn, is not an adventure story like some of the others we have heard. It's a love story. Yes, I see you smiling, Mr. Noah, but soldiers, however fit and fearless, have hearts, too.

We met the lovely lady in this story many years ago when we belonged to a little boy called Walter. Walter, I must say, was a first-class toy-owner. He always put us away in our box at the end of the day and he made sure he lined us up straight when he was playing. That kind of thing is important to a soldier.

However, one day when it was raining hard, Walter noticed that water was pouring through the corner of his ceiling, right above the bed. The roof was leaking.

Of course, there was lots of fuss and bother as grown-ups ran about with buckets. Walter, I'm pleased to say, had more sense. He carefully picked up all the things in his room that he thought were valuable and carried them into his parents' room for safety. We were among the toys, books and clothes he gathered up.

Sometimes I don't know how grown-up people manage to run the world. You would not believe how long it took them to find someone to mend the roof and give Walter his bedroom back.

He had to share a room with his younger brother, but that room was already full of baby toys. We stayed in our new room until the repairs were complete. That is where we met the lovely lady.

One afternoon, tired of being in our box, we marched out for a spot of exercise. "Left, right, left, right, salute!" shouted Sergeant Smith. "Left, right, left, right, present arms!"

We lined up on the carpet. We looked a pretty smart bunch. Next, the Sergeant decided we needed some advanced training. "Climb up the dressing table, capture the hairbrush, and return to this point. You have five minutes!" he yelled.

Within seconds, we were scrambling up the dressing table's twisty legs. I was in the lead, so when I finally hauled myself on to the top, I was the first one to see the lovely lady. I won't pretend otherwise … I was smitten at once.

She was standing in a kind of box, with a mirror behind her, and she wore a beautiful dress of frothy lace. She was the most beautiful lady I had ever seen. One by one, the rest of the unit came to stand beside me. I could tell by their silence that they, too, were overawed by her beauty.

"It's as though she doesn't see us," whispered my old friend Mattie. The lady was looking straight ahead. "Perhaps she's under a spell."

"That only happens in storybooks," I hissed back. "I was thinking she was maybe being held in place by lunar rays or something." (I enjoyed reading science books in my spare time.)

"We might be able to turn them off," said Mattie. "There's a key. Look!" And before I could stop him, he had darted forward and given the key in the front of the box several twists.

It was magical. At once, the most wonderful music began to play, and the lovely lady, bowing her head, began to dance. Around and around she twirled, sometimes lifting one leg gracefully behind her, sometimes raising her beautiful arms above her head. We watched, and we really were under a spell. I had to think again about such storybook ideas.

I was so dazzled by the lovely dancer that I really couldn't think straight, but Sergeant Smith, who had come up to see what had happened to us, frowned.

"I think she's trapped," he said. "Look! She doesn't move from her stand at all. The poor thing is imprisoned in that box!"

The music was slowing down now and becoming softer. Suddenly, the lady herself spoke to us. She was smiling.

"Oh, thank you," she said. "I love to dance. I only come alive when I'm dancing." Then, as the music stopped, it was as if all the life went out of her. She stood still, staring ahead, as if we were not there.

"We have to rescue her!" I whispered. "We can't leave her here like this!"

All my comrades agreed. Gently, they lifted the lady from the box and made a sling from handkerchiefs to lower her to the floor. We carried her carefully back to our box.

"Well done, lads," said Sergeant Smith. "You'll soon feel better, my dear."

But the lovely lady, propped up in front of our box, simply looked straight ahead. She didn't smile, or speak, or dance.

"She needs music!" I cried.

"Come on, men. Our regimental march! One, two, three, four!" called Sergeant Smith. The soldiers began to hum. They put their heart and souls into it. But the lady did not move.

"It's the wrong kind of music!" I cried desperately. Sergeant Smith himself began to sing a love song. We were all astonished to hear what a musical voice he had. Several of us were near to tears when he finished.

But the lady did not move. I thought long and hard as I looked at her lovely face. At last, I had to speak, but I could hardly bring myself to do so.

"She needs…," I whispered. "She needs… She needs her box!"

Sergeant Smith nodded. "I'm afraid you're right, lad," he said. "Come on, let's take her back to where she belongs."

Slowly, we lifted the lady up to the top of the dressing table. We placed her on her stand.

"You do it, lad," said Sergeant Smith.

I turned the key. The music was as beautiful as ever. The lady danced like an angel. She smiled at us all and looked radiantly happy. Then, as the music died, the lady died, too, waiting for the next time that someone would wake her from her sleep. I will never forget her. Never.

The Doll's House Family's Story of

THE TOO-SMALL
HOUSE

told by

MRS. WILBERFORCE HOLLIS

VERY TOUCHING, I'M SURE, SOLDIER, but let's get back to problems in the real world. Magical spells? Dear me! Two bedrooms, a husband, a nanny, and five children— that's what *I* call a problem. And it's exactly what happened to us when our mistress, young Miss Millie, decided to put in a bathroom.

A bathroom! We'd managed, although in cramped conditions, perfectly well with three bedrooms for years. Then Miss Millie's

uncle gave her lots of little bathroom furniture and, of course, she had to put it somewhere. All the children's beds were squeezed into the room that Mr. Hollis and I share or into the nanny's room in the attic.

Well, I don't want to give you the wrong impression, but the Hollis family has never been at all keen on washing. Miss Millie tried to scrub our youngest's face once, and all the baby's paint came off! Poor little mite! No, as a family, we're wary of water, which is why the arrival of the bathroom wasn't very exciting.

There was a big bath on feet, very shiny and very white. There was a washbasin with two taps. And there was a, well, I hardly like to use the word. I shall have to whisper. *A convenience.*

Miss Millie's aunt made some little towels and bars of soap, too. The soap had a most horrible smell, and the baby tried to eat it. It's dangerous stuff to have in a house, if you want my opinion. Those towels were rough, too. More suited to human beings' hard old skin than our delicate paintwork.

Well, I like to think I'm a resourceful woman, so I tried hard to invent other ways to use the bathroom. I made a nice bed for the twins in the bath, but they kept complaining that it was too hard. I tried putting the baby to sleep in the washbasin, but after she fell out the second time, I gave up. I thought the towels might make good doormats, but Miss Millie kept picking them up and putting them back in the bathroom.

In the meantime, no one in the house was getting any sleep. Frankly, it's bad enough sharing a bedroom with Mr. Hollis, who (and I wouldn't tell this to just anyone) snores in a most dreadful way. With three children in there as well, none of whom could put up with the snoring, we all became tired and bad tempered.

There wasn't a moment of the day when the baby wasn't shrieking, the twins weren't squealing, Charles wasn't groaning and Charlotte wasn't moaning.

Then something even more dreadful happened. Miss Maple, who has been the children's nanny since Charlotte was a baby, gave in her notice. Well, I almost fainted away on the spot. I simply don't know what I would do without that woman, who is a *treasure!* She was leaving, of course, because of the impossibly crowded conditions in her little room. I could hardly blame her.

Nevertheless, something had to be done. We needed to get rid of the wretched bathroom—and fast. I spoke to Mr. Hollis about it, and although he was reluctant (something about being worried his top hat might be crushed), when I make up my mind about something, that man doesn't stand a chance.

That night, when Miss Millie was in bed, we crept out and removed the bathroom furniture piece by piece. It took ages to shift the bathtub. There was a lot of heaving and shoving on the stairs with some very bad language from Mr. Hollis and, I'm afraid, Charles. The paintwork is not what it was either.

What, you will ask, did we do with the offending articles? Well, Mr. Hollis had one of his bright ideas, and it did seem pretty good at the time. My husband suggested that we dispose of the bathroom things in the human beings' own bathroom. "Let's flush the wretched things away," said Mr. Hollis.

I can't begin to tell you how difficult it was to hoist the items into position. Dropping them with a satisfying splash was the easy bit. I was in a constant worry in case one of the children or Mr. Hollis himself fell in, but all was happily concluded.

"Now," said Mr. Hollis, "if we all hang onto the chain at the same time, we can flush these things away for ever."

You've never heard such a roaring and a rushing as that contraption made. It was awful. And when we peeped over the edge afterwards, we discovered to our horror that the articles in question were still sitting at the bottom, too heavy to be whooshed away.

Naturally, I gave Mr. Hollis a piece of my mind, but I needn't have worried. When the humans discovered what had happened, Miss Millie's mother forbade her to touch anything that had been in *that place*. Clearly, those things have their uses after all.

The Baby Doll's Story of

THE NAUGHTY LITTLE KITTEN

told by
LITTLE MISS CUDDLES-COO-COO

Coo! Coo! I'M SORRY. I CAN'T HELP IT! I was made to coo and cuddle. I'm supposed to be like a human baby. Coo! Toys are so much more sensible than people. I know I sound silly and babyish but I'm not really. And I know all about difficult animals, too. My story is about a kitten who caused an enormous amount of trouble and a little girl who has a lot to thank me for, although I don't expect she will ever realize it. Anyway, I'll start with the kitten.

I smiled when I heard the China Doll's story about the naughty little puppy. The young animal in my story was even more naughty, but she didn't do it on purpose. In fact, she loved to play and she loved to be cuddled. Well, so do I! Coo! Coo! I couldn't blame her for that.

This kitten—they called her Willow—came into the house when I had lived with my little girl for about a year. At first I was worried, like the China Doll, that my girl would pay more attention to Willow than to me, but I was wrong. In fact, it wasn't long before I felt sorry for that kitten.

You see, my girl loved me very much. She liked to dress me in pretty clothes. She loved to take me out for walks in my own baby carriage. Most of all, she liked to cuddle me and make me say "Coo! Coo!" And when she had a little baby sister, she loved me even more.

"Now we've both got babies," she used to say to her mother. "But mine is the prettiest."

It was a pity that one of the first things the naughty little kitten did was to put her claws into one of my lacy dresses. It did look a bit odd after that, but I really didn't mind. My little girl did. She always liked things to be tidy and pretty.

All the kitten really wanted to do was to play, but my girl didn't understand that. She thought Willow was only interested in scratching and making a mess.

"I don't want a kitten," she told her mother.
My girl's mother was too busy to worry about kittens.

"She was a present from your aunty," she said, "and you must at least pretend to be pleased. And you must look after her, too. It's not enough to give her food and somewhere to sleep. You must play with her, too. She's only a baby herself."

It didn't make any difference to my girl. She preferred to play with *me*. You'd be right to guess I was happy about that. Coo!

But the little kitten wasn't. She got into all kinds of trouble because she was bored and unhappy. Even if she didn't have someone to play with, she loved to cuddle up somewhere warm and go to sleep.

Lots of little girls would love to have a cuddly kitten sleeping on their beds. My girl didn't. She complained to her mother that the kitten left hairs everywhere and scratched when she tried to pick her up.

"I don't have time to worry about it," said her mother. "I've told you before. It's your kitten. You must look after her."

It really wasn't that my girl was cruel. She fed the kitten every day and gave her a basket to sleep in. But she didn't understand that kitten like I did. Coo! Coo!

Now kittens love to curl up in warm places. My girl had put Willow's basket in a dark, cold corner. The kitten didn't like it at all. Willow was always on the lookout for better places to sleep.

My girl's mother threw the kitten out of the warm cupboard where all the linen was kept.

Two days later, she shooed her out of the kitchen, after finding her trying to sleep in the stove! Coo! Once again, she told my girl to take care of the animal. My girl ignored her.

On the morning when it happened, the kitten was dancing around the house as usual, looking for games to play. She knocked over the waste-paper bin and played with balls of paper for a while. Coo!

She tried jumping *down* the stairs ... and landed on her bottom!

She tried jumping *up* the stairs ... did a somersault and landed in a pot plant.

She tried pretending the plant was a jungle and she was a leopard slinking through it. She wasn't very good at slinking yet and left lots of leaves and soil on the carpet.

After all that, the kitten was sleepy and looked around for somewhere warm and snug to cuddle up in.

"Don't come near me!" said my girl, when the kitten rubbed herself against her ankles.

So the kitten went off and found the warmest spot she could—in the baby's cradle. Now, I knew it was dangerous. Kittens can suffocate little children by mistake. I needed to call someone, but what could I do? The only thing I can say that humans can hear is "Coo!" I said it over and over again, as loudly as I could, and I didn't stop.

At last my girl came running into the room.

You know the rest … how my girl was greeted as a heroine for saving her baby sister, how her picture was in the papers, how the famous movie producer spotted her and made her a star.

As for the kitten, she became my greatest friend. You see, my girl soon thought it was babyish to play with dolls now that she was a great actress. Besides, her own little sister wasn't a baby any more. My girl didn't have time for the kitten, either, especially when Willow grew up to become a very charming cat.

But Willow and I got on very well. We played together. We sat together. But best of all, we cuddled up together in the warmest places we could find. Willow was almost as cuddly as I am. After all, I'm not called Little Miss Cuddles-Coo-Coo for nothing. Goodnight!